This Little Tiger
book belongs to:

_____

_____

_____

For my godchildren – Jannis, Ann, Ellen and Lina
~ K S

For Mum, Dad, James and everyone else
behind the scenes
~ L H

LITTLE TIGER PRESS
An imprint of Magi Publications
1 The Coda Centre, 189 Munster Road, London SW6 6AW
www.littletigerpress.com

First published in Great Britain 2005
This edition published 2006

A CIP catalogue record for this book is available from the British Library

Printed in Singapore by Tien Wah Press Pte.

10 9 8 7 6 5 4 3 2 1

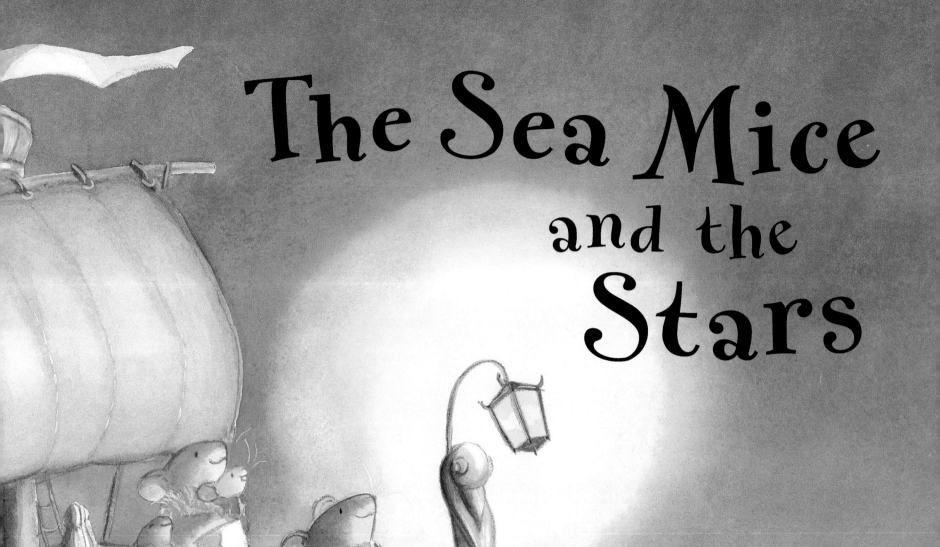

The Sea Mice and the Stars

Kenneth Steven

Illustrated by
Louise Ho

LITTLE TIGER PRESS
London

THE SEA URCHIN

It was winter and the young sea mice
were fast asleep in their boat *The Sea Urchin*.
Outside, snow was falling soft as petals.

Ashenteen woke suddenly.

"Come quickly, little one," her mother Filidore was whispering. "There's something you must see!"

Racing her brother Willabee to the deck, Ashenteen squeaked in amazement. The sky was filled with shooting lights.

"What's happening to the stars?" Ashenteen cried. "Where are they going?"

"Every year," said Uncle Trumble, "as winter comes, there is a shower of falling stars. These stars are pieces of magic, sent to the sea mice to keep us safe. They light our homes and guide us back through storm and snow. It is our family's task to collect them."

Wrapped in their cosy scarves, the mice set
off into the night. The waves leapt and danced
as they rowed to the shore, and Ashenteen
trembled with excitement.

"You must be brave, Pippy," she whispered
to her favourite toy. "We're going on a very
important journey."

At the shore the village mice rushed to welcome them.
"Here are your baskets, Mr Trumble!" said Stigmore.
"But you must hurry, there's a terrible storm coming!"

Uncle Trumble, Filidore, Willabee and Ashenteen struggled up into the snowy hills. The wind howled round them and snowflakes whirled through the dark sky. Ashenteen slipped her paw into Willabee's. This was their very own adventure.

At long last the mice reached a clearing. There lay
hundreds of stars, sparkling like precious jewels in
the snow.

Willabee gasped, his eyes shining.

Ashenteen lifted a glowing shape between both paws.
"Look, Mum!" she squeaked.

"Quickly now!" called Uncle Trumble. "The storm is
getting worse! We must gather all of the stars and go back!"

Ashenteen scampered to
and fro, collecting more
and more stars.

Further and further
she searched, determined
to collect every single one.

"Nearly there," she said, stretching
up into the branches of a tree.

At last she picked the final star from the ground.

"Hello, little star," she murmured, cradling it gently. All around was darkness, but her basket was full to the brim with light.

"We did it!" she whispered proudly.

Filidore put down her basket and looked round for the other mice. "Willabee? Ashenteen?" she called.

"Mum! Mum!" Willabee raced up. "I've found Pippy!" he squeaked. "Ashenteen must have dropped him! I can't find her anywhere!"

"Ashenteen? Ashenteen!" the sea mice called, but there
was no answer.

They peered into the dark and snow. Willabee shivered.
What if Ashenteen was lost for ever? But just then he saw
something flickering faintly in the dark.

"Ashenteen!" Willabee cried. The mice rushed to the glowing light of her basket.

"Thank goodness you're safe!" Filidore said, hugging her youngest mouse close.

Ashenteen beamed with happiness. "I collected every single star!" she murmured.

"Well done, my brave girl," said Filidore proudly.

Uncle Trumble led the mice back through
the wild wind and snow. Ashenteen and Willabee
stumbled on and on, their paws icy cold. At last
they saw the village ahead of them and heard an
excited cry, "You're back!"

The villagers welcomed the sea mice, delighted
to see them safe and sound. Proudly the mice
shared out the stars they had collected – one for
every home.

Then the mice had a great celebration. There were spicy hot drinks that made Ashenteen's nose tingle, and singing and dancing that never seemed to end.

"This is the most exciting night ever!" Ashenteen whispered to Willabee as they nibbled on special star-shaped biscuits, still warm from the oven.

Later the sleepy mice rowed home. The sea was quiet now, and all round the bay the bright new stars shone in the darkness.

Tucked up tight in her bed, Ashenteen gazed at her own special star, blazing out from the prow of the boat. "Good night, Willabee," she whispered, then fell fast asleep, dreaming of the day's great adventure.

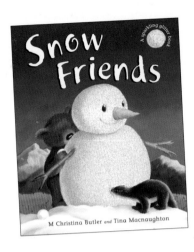

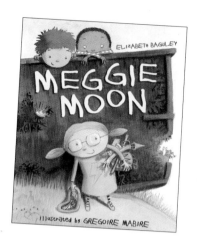

Some more stars from Little Tiger Press

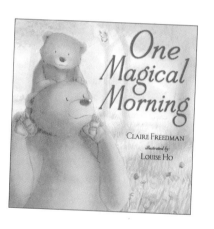

For information regarding any of the above titles
or for our catalogue, please contact us:
Little Tiger Press, 1 The Coda Centre,
189 Munster Road, London SW6 6AW
Tel: 020 7385 6333 Fax: 020 7385 7333
E-mail: info@littletiger.co.uk www.littletigerpress.com